Tough it out, Tom!

Jenny Oldfield

Illustrated by
Neal Layton

a division of Hodder Headline Limited

Thanks for the jokes, George
With grateful thanks to Neal Layton

Text copyright © Jenny Oldfield 2003
Illustrations copyright © Neal Layton 2002
First published in Great Britain in 2003
by Hodder Children's Books

A Catalogue record for this book is available
from the British Library

ISBN 0 340 87757 X

Printed and bound in Great Britain
by Bookmarque Ltd, Croydon, Surrey
*Our grateful thanks to Avocet for providing typesetting
free of charge, and Saxon for providing free cover
reproduction for this edition.*
Paper kindly donated by Norske Skog Union
and Paper Management Services,
printed on Norbook Lux 60gsm/120 microns.

Hodder Children's Books
A Division of Hodder Headline Ltd
338 Euston Road
London NW1 3BH

One

'I must be nice.

I must be nice.

I must be nice.'

Tom stuck his tongue out of the corner of his mouth and scribbled like mad.

'I

I must

I must be

I must be

...Nice, nice, nice!

'Fat chance!' Tom's older brother, Nick, scoffed.

'Shurrup!' Tom said.

'Who gave you the lines, our kid? Was it Rambler Ambler or Witchy Waymann?'

Drop Dead Waymann, the Dread Head.

'I MUST BE NICE.'

Fifty lines, and all because Tom had shoved a beetle under Bex Stevens' stupid, turned-up nose.

It had been lying on its back in the playground, waving its legs around, when Danielle had squealed.

'Aaaagh!'

'What's wrong, Danielle?' Bex had come up to tell her off. Head on one side, hands on hips; 'For goodness sake, it's only a beetle!'

The boys had gathered round.

'Watch out, it's a Grassington Dagger Beetle!' Kingsley had warned.

Wayne had hung back. 'What's one

of them?' he asked.

'Don't listen to 'im!' Ryan had advised. 'It's only a ord'nary cockroach!'

'Aagh!' Danielle had squawked. 'Kill it! Stamp on it! Crush it   to death!'

The helpless beetle had wiggled its legs.

'Don't worry, Beetle, I'll save you!' Super-Tom had dashed in and scooped it off the ground. 'Da-dah!' He'd swung around as if to release the Lesser Spotted Purple People Eater the right way up onto some nice green grass.

'Erk!' Danielle had squeaked. 'He touched it! Tom Bean touched the beetle!'

'Ttttt!' Bex had tossed her head. 'It's only a teeny insect!'

'Yeah, an ickle creepy crawly!' Kingsley had crowed.

'Fancy being scared of that poor little thing!' Bex had rubbed it in.

Then Tom had swung back round with the beetle still between his cupped hands. He'd shoved it right under Bex's nose.

'Aaaaaaagh!' Bex had launched herself into outer space. She'd landed on top of Wayne.

'Hah!' Tom had laughed in her face. 'Who's scared now, huh?'

'Aagh! Aagh! Aagh!' Bex had totally lost it.

So Dob-'em-in Danielle had run off to tell Mrs Waymann. 'Please, miss, it's Tom Bean, miss. He's been horrid again, miss...'

The Head hadn't listened to Tom's excuses.

'Please, miss, it wasn't me, miss. It was Danielle who wanted us to stamp on the beetle. I was the one who saved its life, miss!'

'Fifty lines. "I must be nice." On my desk first thing tomorrow morning.' Waymann had spoken. 'And don't let me catch you in trouble again for the rest of this week, Tom Bean. Or else!'

Tom's lines wiggled like beetles' legs across the page.

'You missed a full-stop!' Nick jeered and stabbed his finger onto the grubby page.

'Gerroff!' Tom tried to snatch the paper away, but it ripped in two.

So Tom jumped up and rugby tackled his big bro. They both crashed down onto the front room carpet, rolled and thumped, kicked and punched until their mum dashed in to referee.

'OK–break it up, you two!' Beth cried.

'Tom started it!' Nick gasped. He got up after landing one last thump.

'He ripped my lines!' Tom jumped to his feet. His face was hot and sweaty.

Frowning, Beth picked up the scraps of paper and slotted them together. '"I must be nice." Hmm.'

'Now I have to start all over again!' Tom moaned.

Nick straightened his tie and tucked in his shirt.

'He's a lunatic, he should be locked up,' he muttered. 'Anyhow, ask him what

he did wrong this time!'

'I didn't do nothin'! I saved a beetle.
'S not my fault if stupid Bex Stevens is
scared of 'em!'

His mum narrowed her eyes. 'I think I'm
beginning to read between the lines!'

Ha-ha, very funny. Not! Tom sulked
in silence.

'All right, I don't want to know the

details!' Beth put her hands up. 'Just get on and do them, Tom. And Nick, leave your brother alone!'

'But I promised I'd meet Kingsley in the park!' Tom whinged. He lunged for his skateboard and baseball cap on the shelf in the hallway.

But his mum got to the door first. 'Oh no, you don't; not tonight!' She poked him with her finger and backed him down the corridor. You sit at this table, young man, and you finish those lines!'

Beth Bean had spoken. She left the room.

'How come I always get the blame?' Tom slumped over the table an hour later.

His writing fingers were sore, but at last he'd managed to write out fifty whole lines. Now he'd come out into his dad's garden shed to have a moan with Chippie.

Tough, dude. The blue budgie had landed on Tom's shoulder and nibbled his ear.

'I mean, they always pick on me, even

when I don't do nothin' wrong.'

Even when I don't do anything wrong, Chippie corrected. *Check it out, dude. I think you'll find I'm right.*

All the other budgies in the shed fluttered and twittered. A new yellow-and-white one did gymnastics from her perch. One forward roll, one dive with tuck, twist and pike, ending in a dive-bomb–neeyah!

'I'm sick of it!' Tom declared. '"Tom, don't do this! Do that! Be quiet! Stand still!" Blah-blah-de-blah! And now Waymann makes me write fifty lines; "I must be nice" blah-blah!!'

Bad day, huh? Peck-peck. The budgie chewed his cheek.

'They're all bad days!'

Tell me about it! Chippie sighed, diving for cover as the yellow-and-white bird whizzed by. *Life's gettin' a little crowded in here!*

Tom puffed out his cheeks then popped them; 'Pwuh!'

They want you to be nice, huh?

'Yeah. Pwuh!'

Meaning what exactly?

'Pwuh-pwuh! Y'know–quiet and goody-goody. Say please and thank you. Pwuh! Don't run in the corridor. Zzzz; boring-snoring!'

Neeyah!

Once more Chippie dodged the dive-bombing newcomer. *Y'know somethin', dude?*

'No; what?' Tom stopped popping his cheeks and paid attention.

You may not like what I'm gonna say about this be-nice gig, but I want you to trust me.

Yeah? Tom tuned in to Chippie's advice.

I mean, they want you to be nice, right?

'Yeah. Ucky-yucky, goo-gooey good!'

Hmm. Chippie considered it, then gave his final verdict. *Why not give it a go, dude?*

'Y'mean; be nice. Be really and truly NICE?' Tom's mouth fell open.

Chippie flew up to his perch. *Yeah, suck it and see,'* he said. *'Who knows? It could be a blast!*

TWO

'Tum-tum-te-tum!' Tom hummed in the shower. He splished and splashed, soaped and lathered, then sprayed himself clean.

His mum knocked on the bathroom door. 'Tom, is that you?' she asked in a shocked voice.

'Yup!' he replied.

'Who ordered you to have a shower? Was it your dad?'

'Nope.' Tom emerged with a towel around his waist. 'It was my idea.'

'B-b-but! You never go anywhere near water!' Beth was white with shock as she followed Tom into his bedroom. 'Good lord!' she gasped.

'Whassup?'

Tom's mum gazed around the room. 'You've tidied up!'

He opened his sock drawer to show her the neatly rolled-up pairs. 'Da-dah!'

'I c-c-can see the carpet!' Beth rubbed her eyes in disbelief. 'And you've made your own bed!'

'Look!' Tom showed her his wardrobe. 'Everything's hung up on hangers.'

'I'd better sit down!' She plonked on his bed.

'Watch out, you'll crease the duvet!' Tom pulled her up again. 'What's wrong? D'you feel sick? Let me make you a nice cuppa!'

Sprinting downstairs, he turned on the kettle.

His mum followed more slowly. 'OK, Tom, you can drop the act,' she told him. 'Just give it to me straight; what do you want?'

'Nothin'!' he protested.

'Yes, you do. You're after a new skateboard!'

Dangling a tea bag into a mug of hot water, Tom shook his head. 'Listen, I gotta go and get dressed or I'll be late for school.'

'Not so fast!' Beth grabbed his skinny arm. 'What happened to the Tom-my-middle-name-is-trouble-Bean that I know and love?'

Tom slithered free. 'That was then, this is now!' Tum-te-tum! He skipped upstairs.

'You mean you've turned over a new leaf?' Beth yelled.

Tom squirmed into his trousers and shirt. 'Yep!'

'I don't believe you. Is this a joke?' And yet Beth Bean had the evidence in front of her eyes in the shape of a super-tidy son.

Tom appeared squeaky-clean at the top

of the stairs. 'It's true!' he claimed. 'Since I got given those lines, I've thought it through. No more Mr Nasty; from now on I'm gonna be n-i-c-e, NICE!'

Straight away Tom put his and Chippie's plan into action.

On the bus to school he looked around for a little old lady to give up his seat to. He said thank you to the driver when he let him and Kingsley off at their stop, then he waved cheerfully at the school crossing man. He even tried to be nice to Bex Stevens and her gang.

'Hey, Bex, did you know that the zip on your bag is broken?' he asked her in the playground.

Teachers' pet Bex frowned, checked her gaping bag, then turned round and accused Tom. 'OK, I suppose you think that unzipping my bag is funny!'

He shook his head. 'All I did was let you know, in case somebody came along and nicked something.'

'Yeah, yeah, pull the other one, Tom Bean! It must have been you sneaking up and opening it; how else could it have happened?'

Yeah, Tom!' Danielle and Sasha chimed in.

He was just about to argue back when he heard Chippie's chirpy voice saying: *Don't rise to it, dude. Chill out and walk away.*

So he did.

Then he went and opened a door for Miss Ambler.

'Why thank you, Tom!' The new teacher nearly dropped her pile of books in surprise.

After that, he took his lines to the Head.

'Put them down on my desk!' Waymann barked without looking up.

Tom obeyed and tiptoed out of her office, slap-bang into Bernie King, the caretaker, and his fat bulldog, Lennox. Bernie eyed Tom suspiciously, then barged in to Waymann's room.

'I'm looking for volunteers to do litter duty at morning break,' he told her.

Tom jumped in. 'I'll do it!' he vowed.

Bernie and Waymann's mouths fell open.

'Maybe I'd better get my lugs cleaned out,' Bernie muttered. 'I could've sworn I just heard Tom Bean say he'd do it!'

'I did. I will!' Tom promised.

Wicked, dude! Chippie's voice said. *Look at his face!*

The caretaker's jaw had dropped so far it had practically hit the ground. Tom grinned.

Fat Lennox growled.

Waymann and the King of Woodbridge Junior just gawped.

'Tsk! look at Tom showing off!' Danielle hissed at Sasha when Tom offered to wipe the whiteboard for Mr Wright.

Squeak-squeak–Tom rubbed it clean.

Thank you, Thomas!' Leftie murmured. Who is this polite, helpful pupil, I wonder? I'm not sure I've met him before!'

Tom blushed. Being nice was turning out to be a major effort.

'Sir, did you see 'im collecting litter in the playgound?' Kingsley piped up.

'Yeah, and he carried some chairs for Miss Ambler, then he took the afternoon registers round for Mrs Hannam!' Dob-'em-in Danielle chimed in.

Leftie gave Tom a curious look. There was another pause, then a penny seemed to drop. 'I get it! There's money in it for you if you get through a whole day without being told off!'

Tom looked peeved. 'No, sir!' He scowled at Danielle, then pulled himself up short.

(Nice one, dude. Keep 'em guessing!)

'This is the real me, sir. And I swear I'm never gonna crack another joke or play another trick in my whole life!'

'Boring!' Kingsley groaned at the school gates.

'Yeah, boring!' Ryan agreed. He went

off, arms spread wide, to fly his Spitfire into the face of enemy fire. Neeyah!

Ack-ack-ack! He zapped a Messerschmidt, then, banking steeply, he flew back to join them.

'Why are you doing it, Tom?' Wayne asked. 'Why are you being so yucky?'

Tom shrugged. 'Dunno. Just feel like it.'

Kingsley folded his arms and leaned against the gate post. 'Yeah, but it's weird!' he pointed out. 'We like it when you hide the registers from Hannam, not take 'em round, all organised like you're Bex or somebody!'

'Yeah!' Ryan agreed. 'You're like Bex! Ack-ack-neeyah!

'Yeah! It's just not you.' Even shy Wayne was disappointed.

Then Bernie King came up with Fat Lennox at his heels. 'OK, the game's up. You're not fooling anyone with this goody-goody act, Tom Bean!'

'What? Why?' Tom backed off as

Lennox slavered over his trainers.

'What are you up to?' Bernie quizzed.
His stubbly chin jutted out and his stubbly
hair stood up from his head.

'Nothing!' Tom spread his hands,
resisting an urge to kick Lennox in the
slobbery chops.

Stay cool, dude. Don't blow it.

Bernie sneered at his answer. 'I wouldn't

trust you as far as I could throw you!'

Hrrrughh! Lennox growled. Me neither.

'Stupid mutt!' Tom muttered under his breath.

Don't blow it, dude. I'm serious!

'What did you just say?' Bernie snapped.

'I said, "Ouch; my foot!"' Tom lied.

Kingsley, Ryan and Wayne sniggered.

Lennox sank his fangs into Tom's trouser leg and began to shake his head viciously.

Tom let out another insult. 'Leggo, you big slob!'

(Man, I give up. I'm outta here!)

'Say that again!' Bernie challenged.

Tom took a deep breath. He shut his eyes and tried to squeeze the words back down his throat. But they fought back and leaped out in a mad cry. 'LEGGO, YOU BIG SLOB!!!'

He'd blown it. No more Mr Nice Guy!

'Hah!' Bernie shouted triumphantly. 'I knew it couldn't last!'

'Hurrah!' Wayne, Kingsley and Ryan cried.

'Let 'im 'ave it, Tom!'

And Tom let rip. 'Leggo of my foot, you big heap of doggy doo-doo!'

Lennox clamped his jaws tighter still. He held on like a heavyweight wrestler as Tom lifted his leg and swung him through the air.

'Put that dog down!' Bernie insisted.

Tom shook his leg and tried to dump the dog.

Hrruff! Lennox lost his grip and landed with a splat. Bernie rushed forward to rescue his pet. 'Just you wait until I tell the Head!' he cried.

Tom gazed down at his shredded trousers. 'Look; my mum's gonna kill me!'

'No change there, then,' Kingsley grinned.

'You kicked my dog!' Bernie yelled.

'Your dog bit me!' Tom was boiling with anger. Even the sight of Leftie wheeling his Yamaha out of the bike shed didn't shut him up.

'Lennox is trained not to bite people!'

Bernie insisted. 'He wouldn't harm a fly!'

Tom hopped up and down, waving his shredded trousers in the air. 'What did this then? A bunch of hungry midgies?'

'Yeah!' the gang cried. 'Right on, Tom!'

No word from Chippie, though.

'Er-hum!' It was Leftie in his shiny black crash helmet who interrupted the argument. 'Tom, calm down.'

'Sir, it wasn't me...!'

'I said, calm down.' The young teacher shook his head. 'I want you to go home and tidy yourself up, come back tomorrow in a better mood, OK?'

''S not fair!' Tom muttered.

Meanwhile, Bernie and Lennox looked on with satisfaction.

'Same old Tom Bean,' Bernie snorted. 'Fighting and lying and causing trouble as usual. I knew it! A leopard can't change its spots!'

'Sir!'

'Go!' Leftie ordered.

"'S not flippin' fair!' Mumbling and grumbling, hanging his head and leading Kingsley, Ryan and Wayne out of the school grounds, Tom went on his way.

'Everybody better watch out!' he grunted, thinking *No more Mister Nice Guy*. Tomorrow he would be as bad as he'd ever been in his life.

Oh, and he planned to have a stern word with Chippie too. 'This is all down to you, Chip!' he muttered to himself.

But there was silence. Not a word from the bird.

Three

'So, you see, no way did it go according
to plan!'

Tom had scoffed his sausages and beans,
slurped his pears and custard, then dashed
out to the shed.

'I try to be nice and I end up in more
trouble!' He leaned against the door, arms
folded across his chest. Chippie gazed at
him from his perch.

'For instance, what's so flippin' great about picking up litter? Sure, Bernie and Waymann were gobsmacked, but that only lasted ten seconds. Same with my mum. Now she'll be expecting me to have showers every single morning!'

Chippie sat huddled on his perch without saying anything. He puffed out his chest feathers and let his head droop.

'And y'know what?' Tom went on. 'Kingsley said I was borin'! He said I was acting like Bex. I mean, that's scary. Me, like Bex Stevens!'

He paused for this to sink in. Then he began to grin. 'Tell you what, though, you should have seen Bernie's face when I called Lennox a big pile of doggy doo-doo, which he is. Bernie nearly had a heart attack. Then me and the gang ran off to the park. We skimmed stones in the river and I got home dead late. Mum went mad and told Dad. Now I'm grounded for the rest of the week.'

Tom sighed happily. Things were back to normal. Then he realised: Chippie had not said a word. Not a dickie bird. Come to think of it, the budgie wasn't even flying up to him and perching on his head.

'Are you in a strop with me?' he asked, going closer. 'I'm only saying being nice for the day wasn't worth it. I'm not blaming you or anything!'

Chippie hunched lower. He blinked a bleary eye.

'C'mon!' Tom coaxed. 'I'm not saying it wasn't a good idea.'

Silence. Chippie sat like a dischuffed sparrow caught in the rain.

'OK, OK, so maybe I didn't give it a proper chance,' Tom admitted. 'And yeah, I blew it when Fat Lennox sank his teeth into me. I admit that.'

Chippie's eyes drooped wearily. *Man, leave it out. Let me get some sleep.*

Tom looked more closely. It wasn't like the bird to be so quiet. 'Whassup,

Chip?' he murmured.

Chippie shut his eyes and refused to answer.

And now Tom was worried. Chirpy Chippie wasn't chirpy any more. Grumpy, more like. Yeah, definitely moody. To Tom this could only mean one thing.

'Are you sick?' he asked anxiously.

Silence. Meanwhile the new yellow-and-white budgie started a scrap with two others over a manky piece of cuttlefish. Feathers flew and the squawks reached Harry Bean out in the garden.

Tom's dad came to the rescue. He entered the aviary, picked up the cuttlefish, dusted it down and re-fixed it between some wire mesh. Then he took some fresh pieces from the cupboard, so that each bird could peck at the treat without having to fight.

'There!' he said, brushing seed husks from his hands. 'That yellow one's certainly taking his time to settle in.'

'I thought it was a her,' Tom muttered,

still studying Chippie and wondering what was wrong.

'So did I when I bought him, but then I took a closer look, and "she" is a "he"!'

Tom tutted. 'What's his name?'

'Dunno. What d'you think?' Harry stooped under the low, sloping roof, his gangly figure taking up most of the space. 'I was thinking maybe Dave...Tom?'

'Hmm? What?' Yep, there was definitely something up with Chippie. 'Dad, will you take a look at Chip? I think he's sick.'

'Why, what's he been up to?' Gently Harry took the budgie between his giant cupped hands. He stroked him with his thumb and smoothed his wing feathers before he put him back on his perch.

'Just sittin' there,' Tom explained. 'Not talking or anything.'

'Maybe he's having an off day. Birds are just like people; they have bad moods, too.'

Tom frowned. 'What if he's not eating his seed? Will he starve?'

'Eventually, but I don't think you need to worry yet.'

'What else can happen if a budgie's not well?' Tom wanted to know. 'I mean, can they get flu and measles and stuff?'

Harry hid a smile. 'Chippie's not likely to come out in a rash, if that's what you mean.'

'Maybe he's got a temperature!' Tom

started to think of all the awful possibilities. 'Can they have heart attacks and stuff?'

Harry took Tom by the arm and led him out of the shed.

'Calm down, son,' he advised. 'And don't panic. I've taken a look at Chippie and as far as I can see, there's nothing to worry about!'

Tom nodded. Yeah, he was being stupid. Chippie was just in a mood with him over the being-nice thing.

He tiptoed back to look through the window. He saw Chippie pecking at a dish of food and spitting out the husks, then new boy Dave dive-bombing in to shove Chippie off his perch.

Chippie hopped away to a safe distance to sulk and ruffle his feathers some more.

Yeah, Tom thought, Chippie was having a bad hair day.

Course he wasn't sick...was he?

Four

'I'm glad to see that things are back to normal, Tom!' Leftie remarked to Tom on Wednesday lunchtime. Tom had already been in trouble three times; once from Leftie for flicking soggy paper pellets at Danielle during maths; once from Miss Ambler for getting 'lost' when he went to the toilet; and now the call had come for him to go to Waymann's office.

'The Head wants to have a little word with Tom Bean about last night,' Bex reported. 'Mrs Hannam asked me to pass on the message.'

'Having a little word' was Waymann's way of striking terror into every pupil's heart. It meant standing by her desk to get an ear-bashing, plus weeks of detention and hundreds of lines for doing somthing minor like sticking bubble gum on Danielle's chair. Tom knew this because Waymann had 'little words' with him most weeks at school.

So Leftie's joky comment didn't raise a smile. In fact, Tom hung his head like a condemned man as he made his way down the corridor to the Head's room, and he ignored his teacher's query about what had gone wrong now.

'It'll be about the names he called Lennox last night!' Bernie King jumped in with the accusations. The caretaker had come round a corner and almost bumped in to Tom. 'I reported him first thing this morning.'

'Ah yes, there was some name-calling going on,' Leftie murmured. 'But as I recollect, Tom was provoked.'

'Yeah!' Tom pouted. 'Lennox was only mangling my left leg at the time!'

Burly Bernie bristled. 'Let's see what the Head has to say!' he snorted, storming ahead to knock loudly on the dark brown door.

Leftie gave Tom a nudge. 'Don't worry, I'll act as your witness,' he promised.

'Come!' The Head's voice boomed through the door.

Bernie flung it open and marched in. 'There's someone to see you, Mrs Waymann.'

Waymann glared at her three visitors over the top rim of her glasses. 'Not you again!' she sighed when she saw Tom.

'Remember, I told you; he called Lennox bad names!' Bernie barked.

Trembling but determined, Tom launched his counter attack.

'Only 'cos Lennox wouldn't let go of my leg! I'd been mega nice to people all day, then he comes along and rips my trousers to bits!'

'I'll vouch for that,' Leftie chipped in. 'I happened to be there, Mrs Waymann.

The Dread Head stared straight through the junior teacher.

'That's no excuse for calling the poor animal rude names,' she said severely.

'He's not a poor animal. He's a savage, slavering, slobby mutt!' Tom burst out.

He expected to hear Chippie's voice saying, *Woah, dude! Chill out. Don't lose your cool, man.* But nothing came through to him.

Waymann sighed and rose from her seat. A cloud of flowery perfume wafted Tom's way. 'Need we say any more?' she said primly to Leftie. 'I think that Tom has just nicely proved Mr King's case against him.'

'Talk about putting your foot in it!' Leftie murmured to Tom, while Bernie rubbed his hands in satisfaction.

'My dog wouldn't harm a fly,' he insisted. 'He's been properly trained only to react when someone threatens either him or me. Then its only natural for him to protect himself.'

Mrs Waymann listened and reached her verdict. She scribbled a few words on a piece of paper then handed it to Tom. 'Write this one hundred times!' she ordered. 'I want it first thing in the morning!'

'I must be nice to Lennox.
I must be nice to
I must be nice
I must be'

'Back to normal, I see,' Beth sighed as she passed the table where Tom was working.

'Huh!' he grunted, tongue sticking out of the corner of his mouth.

'Let's have a gander!' Nick cried. He'd dashed in from the yard where he'd been fixing the chain on his bike. Grabbing Tom's paper with his oily mitts, he laughed out loud.

'Give us it!' Tom yelped. He lunged at Nick and grabbed the paper. 'Now look what you did!'

'Stop it, you two!' Beth was on autopilot, too busy with cooking burgers and chips to pay much attention.

So Tom and Nick had a quick scrap which ended in Nick screwing up Tom's lines and Tom stomping outside to the shed.

''S not fair!' he glowered, ducking as Dave screeched by.

The other birds seemed to be keeping well out of the way of the newcomer, clinging to the wire mesh walls and quietly minding their own business.

Dave swooped and wheeled around, then made an emergency landing on Tom's head.

Tom felt the yellow budgie's feet dig straight through his cap into his scalp. Good job I've got loads of hair! he thought.

Meanwhile, Dave tweaked and pecked, pulling strands out one by one.

'Ouch!' Tom whisked Dave off and looked around for Chippie. 'I've got a mega problem,' he muttered, casting his gaze over the rows of birds at the food dishes. 'Chip, where are you? I need to talk!'

No reply.

'C'mon, stop messing around. You can't still be mad at me.' Tom searched in corners and even on the floor. 'Chip, don't be stupid!'

Neeyah! Dave broke the sound barrier as he zoomed past.

Dude, I'm over here, a small voice sighed.

Squinting into a dark corner, Tom at last picked out Chippie's hiding place. His favourite budgie was huddled on a narrow ledge above the cupboard where Harry Bean stored the bags of birdseed. The moment he spotted him, Tom's heart missed a beat. Then he moved swiftly across the shed. 'What's up?' he asked anxiously, stretching his arm for Chippie to hop onto his finger.

The bird hunched down further. *Don't hassle me, dude. Just give me a little alone-time, huh?*

'Are you still feeling sick?' Tom asked. He opened the cupboard to pull out a stool, which he stood on to take a closer look at Chippie. 'I thought you'd be better by now.'

Yeah, dude. But I'm not myself, that's for sure.

Tom could see that this was true. The budgie looked even worse than yesterday; thin and peaky, with two bald patches on his chest. 'You're losing your feathers!' he gasped.

Yeah, man. I'm moulting big time.

'Why? What's happening?' Tom felt the panic form a knot in his stomach.

Don't ask! Chippie blinked.

Neeyah! Dave made another mad raid, this time into Chippie's dark corner. Chip squeezed himself into the furthest angle and tried to make himself invisible.

'I've got it!' Tom cried. 'Dave's bullying

you! He won't let you near your food.
He's pecking you to bits and pulling out
your feathers!'

Keep your voice down, dude.

'That's it!' Tom was convinced. 'Listen,
I'll talk to Dad. I'll tell him Dave's being
a big pest!'

No way. Don't rock the boat.

Zooooom! The yellow bird flashed by.
Then he turned, circled around Tom's head,
banked and swooped away.

'Yeah!' Tom hissed. 'This is serious.
You'll be bald by the end of the week if
this goes on!'

Very attractive, huh? Chippie replied
mournfully.

'We gotta get Dave out of here!' Tom
decided. 'Dad will have to give him back to
the man he bought him from.'

Dave landed on a vacant perch,
puffed out his chest and smoothed his
wing feathers. *I'm the main man. Don't
mess with me!*

Don't mess with him, Chippie warned Tom.

But Tom was worried sick. What happens if we don't say something to Dad?' he appealed to his bullied pal. 'Dave gets away with it and you starve to death!'

I say cool it, you hear me?

Tom frowned. He stroked Chippie's head with his forefinger.

'Is there something you're not telling me?' he pleaded. He wondered exactly what went on in the aviary when there was no one here to stand guard. How bad was Dave? How mean and nasty did he get with the other birds?

Puhh-lease, dude, don't ask. Chippie shifted uneasily on the ledge. Listen, do me a favour and tough this one out, huh?

'What d'you mean, tough it out?' Tom huffed and puffed, scratched his head and tried to work it out. 'Why can't I tell Dad?'

Because! Chippie insisted. He puffed out what was left of his feathers and closed his weary eyes. *Chill!* he told Tom.

Just don't say a word, OK?

'I promise!' Tom agreed at last.

Cool! Chip's eyelids flickered open and he gave Tom a grateful look.

Then the bird fell fast asleep.

Five

K...L...M. M for Moulting.

Carefully Tom looked up the word in Harry's 'Budgies as Pets' book.

The night before, he'd left his chips and burgers uneaten on his plate, then gloomily said no to an invite from Kingsley to go down the park.

'Whaddyamean, "no"!' Kingsley had cried. 'You always come skateboarding with us!'

Tom's noisy friend had ignored his grumpy protests and dragged Tom off. But Tom's heart wasn't in it. He'd messed up his kickflips and bodged his pop shove-its. Twice he'd landed on his bum.

'Nice bail, Tom!' Kingsley had crowed.

Tom's board had shot off solo–click-whir-click–smack into a tree. Tom had just sat there feeling sorry for himself.

All of a sudden, pulling off wicked ollies and grinds had lost its appeal. 'I'm off home,' he'd grunted, taking off his baseball cap and trudging home with his dented board.

He'd gone to bed early and hardly slept a wink. Then he'd nodded off after the alarm had gone, got up late and dived for his dad's reference book.

"Moulting". He found the entry and began to read. "There are several reasons why a bird may lose its feathers..."

'Cheer up, Tom!' Beth told him as she lifted the book he was reading to

wipe the kitchen table.

'Hey!' he yelped.

Beth glanced at the book and put it back on the shelf. 'No time for reading. You've got to get ready for school.'

'But Mum!'

'No buts. Shower please, and double-quick!'

Moaning and groaning, he trailed upstairs. He turned on the shower, put a toe under the jet, then scarpered into his bedroom and struggled into yesterday's crumpled clothes.

'Tom, you're late!' his mum yelled from the bottom of the stairs.

He shot down, heading straight for the shed.

Beth put out an arm to grab him. 'Oh no you don't!'

'Yeah! I've gotta give Chippie his breakfast!' Tom protested.

'Your dad did it before you got up.' Beth thrust his school bag into his arms and steered him towards the front door. 'Go on, scoot!'

'B-b-but!'

'No buts. School!'

And so Tom did as he was told, feeling the worry about his bird rest like a stone in his empty stomach.

Thursday. The longest day.

'Whassup?' Kingsley asked during morning break.

'Nothin'.' Tom felt dazed. All he could think about was Chippie.

'Tom, come and play footie!' Wayne invited, trotting by with a ball tucked under his arm.

It had begun to drizzle and Tom had taken shelter in the bike shed.

'No thanks,' he said glumly.

Kingsley squared up to him. 'What is this?' he demanded. 'First you flunk the kickflips, now you say no to footie. Are you feeling pukey?'

Tom shook his head, then took a deep breath. 'No, but Chippie is,' he confessed.

Kingsley leaned his head to one side. 'The bird is sick?' he checked.

'Yeah, he won't eat. And he's losing his feathers.' Overcome by the urge to share his worries, Tom laid out the whole problem to his friend. 'Dave's been bullying him.'

'Who's Dave?'

'He's like a mafia budgie moving in on new turf,' Tom explained, tears welling up in his eyes. 'All the others are dead scared of getting in his way, and he's picking on Chippie to show how tough he is.'

Kingsley listened then grinned. 'So why is the bird bald?'

'Dave is pullin' his feathers out!' Tom declared. 'He tried it with my hair, only I wouldn't let him.'

'This Dave,' Kingsley said, 'he sounds like the budgie version of Fat Lennox!'

Scowling at the bulldog across the yard, Tom nodded. 'I'm dead worried about

Chippie, but he won't let me tell Dad.'

Kingsley gave Tom a weird look. 'I'm gonna pretend you never said that last bit,' he muttered. Then he turned to Ryan and a gang of boys who were heading for the footie game. 'Hey, listen to this! Tom's budgie is going bald!'

'Whoo-hoo!' the gang cried. 'What does a budgie look like in the nude?'

Tom turned away, only to see Bex, Sasha and Danielle standing at the side of the bike shed. 'What're you staring at?' he challenged, swallowing back the tears.

'Nothing!' the girls chorused, while Kingsley ran off to join Ryan.

'Is your budgie really going bald?' Danielle demanded.

'What's it to you?' Tom was fed up. The last thing he needed was a grilling from the girls.

But then Bex stepped in with a message from the Head.

Suddenly Tom remembered one hundred

"I must be nice to Lennox" lines. 'Don't tell me; Waymann would like a little word!' Bex nodded. She could tell by his face that he hadn't done them.

'Say your budgie's sick,' Danielle advised. 'Maybe she'll let you off.'

Tom gave a hollow laugh. With his head hanging and hands in his pockets, he slouched off for his first telling off of the day.

'I must not make silly excuses.
I must not make silly
I must not make
I must not ~~not~~'

Rats! Tom crossed out the second 'not'. It was a wet lunchtime and he was stuck in a corner of the dining hall writing out two hundred lines. From across the busy room, his mum was clearing dinner tables and looking suspiciously in his direction.

Tom was so busy hiding what he was

doing that he didn't feel Dob-'em-in
Danielle sneak up on him.

'What did you tell Waymann?' she
demanded.

'The truth.'

('Please, miss, my brother smudged oil all
over them!' 'Tom Bean, that is the silliest
excuse I've ever heard!')

Although Tom hid his paper from
Danielle, she still hovered stubbornly
nearby. Clearing her throat, she took a
small card from her pocket and offered
it to him. 'I made this for you.'

Tom narrowed his eyes. What was this;
some kind of trick?

'Go on, take it!' Danielle insisted, her face
red and her voice quieter than usual. 'It's a
card saying I'm sorry about Chippie.'

'Whitty-woo!' Ryan ran by jeering. 'Tom
Bean fancies Danielle!' he cawed.

'Naff off!' Tom hissed at Ryan. 'Listen,
if this is a wind up...'

'It isn't! Go on, take it.'

So he took the card while a crowd gathered round.

'Tom's going out with Danielle!' they hooted. 'Whitty-woodle-woo!'

'So Sorry!' Tom read on the front of the home-made card. The letters were surrounded by daisies. Inside there was a drawing of a blue bird sitting on a perch decorated with pink ribbons, and the words, 'Get well soon. Luv from Danni'.

'You should've seen your face!' Kingsley had been laughing at Tom all the way home.

''S not funny!' After the shock of Danielle's card, the day had dragged. Now all Tom wanted to do was hop off the bus and run to find out how Chippie was doing.

'It's mega hilarious!' Kingsley's guffaw echoed up and down the street. 'I mean, I'm serious; Danielle fancies you! How funny is that!'

Tom went pale at the idea. 'You gotta help me!' he begged.

'No way. It's a mega-laugh.' Hooting with laughter, Kingsley ran on to the park.

Slowly Tom went up his own path. As he dumped his bag in the hallway, he heard that his postman dad was already back from work.

'I'm worried about Dave and how he's settling in,' Harry confessed to Beth.

Tom stopped outside the kitchen door.

'Why, what's wrong?' Beth asked.

'Well, he's kind of hyper-active; just not what I expected.'

'Considering you thought he was a she, I can see your point!' Beth chuckled.

There was a long pause, then Harry said, 'I left a message with Jason, asking his advice. I'm waiting for him to get back to me.'

'Yes!' Tom clenched his fist in a silent cheer. Jason must be the man they'd bought Dave from. His dad would talk to Jason and decide to hand Dave back. Dave's reign in the Bean aviary would

be over and Chippie's life would be saved!
With his thoughts sprinting ahead, Tom
burst into the kitchen. 'We-gotta-get-rid-of'-
im!' he gabbled, cannoning into the table
and sliding underneath.

Harry dragged him out. 'Steady on!' As
he dusted Tom down, he saw that tears of
relief were streaming down his son's face.

'Whoah, what's going on?'

'I told you Chippie was sick!' Tom gasped.
'Well, he is. He's starvin' and moultin', but

I couldn't say anything...it was torture,
but Chippie wouldn't let me...'

'Hold your horses!' Beth said. 'Harry, I
haven't a clue what's going on, but I think
you'd better take Tom out to the shed and
get to the bottom of things.

Harry nodded. 'Don't cry, son,' he said
gently, as they crossed the garden.

'I don't want him to be dead already!'
Tom wailed. It was no good, he just couldn't
tough it out any longer.

Harry lifted the latch and ushered Tom
inside the shed. Together they stood and
waited for the fluttering budgies to settle
back on their perches.

White, yellow, grey, green and blue birds
flew hither and thither. The sound of tiny
beating wings filled the air.

Divebomb Dave crash-landed in a water
dish with a splash.

'Where's Chippie?' Harry whispered.

'He was on the ledge over the cupboard,'
Tom replied, hardly daring to breathe. If

Dave had gone on pecking and pestering Chippie, he would–well, he didn't know what he would do!

Harry was the first to venture into the dark corner. 'Yes, here he is!' he murmured. 'Come on, Tom; stand on the stool and help me take a closer look!'

'Let him be still alive!' Tom breathed. He climbed onto the stool. 'Be OK, Chip! Please be OK!'

'Hmm!' Harry said as he studied Chippie.

Hey! Tom came eye to beady eye with his bird. Not dead, then! 'How d'you feel?' he asked.

Totally cool, dude, Chippie said perkily.

Tom stared. 'Y'mean, you're better!' He made tweeting noises to encourage the budgie to hop onto his finger.

'How's he look to you?' Harry inquired.

'He's still a bit bald and he's not moving from the spot.'

Tom didn't get it. Again he tweeted, but once more Chippie refused to budge.

Less of the tweety stuff, man! the bird said testily. *I ain't moving; not for anyone.*

'Listen, there's no need to be scared of Dave any more,' Tom explained. 'Dad's gonna talk to Dave's ex-owner. We're gonna send him back, aren't we, Dad?'

'Maybe,' Harry said slowly, reaching up to the ledge.

'Er-hum, Tom, can you lean back a bit?'

'No, don't touch him, Dad!' Tom warned. 'He won't like it!'

Back off, dude! Chippie squawked.

But Harry was determined. Closing his big hand over the tiny bird, he gently lifted Chippie clear of his ledge.

What?...How? Tom stared and gulped. There on the narrow shelf lay a small, perfectly formed pale blue egg.

'She was a he and he was a she!' Tom hopped around the lawn, bursting with excitement.

His mum stood next to his dad.

'Come again?' she said.

'We just found out that Chippie isn't a he, he's a she!' Tom cried. 'After all this time, it turns out that Chip can lay eggs!'

(Why the big surprise, man. I told you I wasn't myself!)

'Never!' Beth laughd.

Tom nodded. 'He-she wasn't sick after all. She was just broody and down in the dumps, trying to lay her very first egg!'

(Put me down, dude. Let me get on with hatching this baby!)

Beth's eyebrows shot up. 'Well, that's very -er-nice-isn't it?' She went off quickly to answer a knock at the front door.

'It's mega!' Tom confirmed happily. Chippie wasn't going to die. She was going to be a mother!

Harry smiled at Tom. 'Life's full of surprises,' he said.

'It's Jason, about the problem with Dave,' Beth announced, coming back into the garden, followed by a man and a girl.

The man came forward. 'I hear she's a bit too lively for you,' Jason began.

'She's a he,' Harry informed him.

But Tom wasn't listening any more. He was staring at Danielle. 'How? What? Who?' he gasped again.

'Tom, close your mouth!' Beth reminded him.

'Jason's my dad,' Danielle explained with a sickly sweet smile.

Oh No! Tom recognised that look on a girl's face. He gritted his teeth and backed away.

'Tom, I was wondering...' Danielle simpered. 'I mean, would you show me - erm - teach me properly how to skateboard in the park?'

No. No way! Double-double-negative! I'd rather cook in a cauldron of boiling oil!
'Maybe,' he muttered weakly.

Danielle giggled. 'Now?' she wheedled.

Quickly Tom got his act together. 'Can't, not now,' he gasped.

Danielle's brow creased. 'Aw, why not?'

'I'm busy.'

'Doing what?'

'Writing lines for Waymann!' he shot
back. 'The ones you dobbed me in about
in the first place!'

'Huh!' Danielle went into a strop.
No more Miss Sickly Sweet. She stomped
off to the park alone.

'I must not make
I must not make silly
I must not make silly excuses,' Tom wrote.

His hand ached. He'd used up a whole green biro. But he didn't care. Chippie was gonna be around for a whole lot longer, and soon there would be-yep- a chip off the old block!

Carefully Tom counted the lines-196, 197, 198, 199, 200!